Vanished!

Phoebe looked as if she was about to cry. "I spent a really long time writing a super-cool ending for our mystery story," she said miserably. "And now the whole story is gone!"

"We'll find the notebook," Nancy told her.

Nancy and Phoebe retraced Phoebe's path from their classroom to her cubby to the playground. Bess and George looked in the lunchroom and the bathroom and the trashcans. But the notebook was nowhere to be found.

"There are only two things that could have happened to it," Nancy pointed out. "Either you lost it, or . . ." Her voice trailed off.

"Or someone stole it," Bess finished.

"Right. And if someone stole it, we'll have to find the thief," Nancy said. "Our mystery story is turning into a *real* mystery."

The Nancy Drew Notebooks

Available from MINSTREL Books

THE
NANCY DREW
NOTEBOOKS®

#36

The Make-Believe Mystery

CAROLYN KEENE
ILLUSTRATED BY JAN NAIMO JONES

A MINSTREL® BOOK

Published by POCKET BOOKS
New York   London   Toronto   Sydney   Singapore

This book is a work of fiction. Names, characters, places and incidents are products of the author's imagination or are used fictitiously. Any resemblance to actual events or locales or persons living or dead is entirely coincidental.

A MINSTREL PAPERBACK *Original*

A Minstrel Book published by
POCKET BOOKS, a division of Simon & Schuster Inc.
1230 Avenue of the Americas, New York, NY 10020

ISBN: 0-671-04267-X

First Minstrel Books printing June 2000

10 9 8 7 6 5 4 3 2 1

Cover art by Joanie Schwarz

Printed in the U.S.A.

PHX/✶

1
The Contest

"Class, I have a special project for you," Mrs. Reynolds announced. She reached into her desk drawer and pulled out a brown paper bag.

Eight-year-old Nancy Drew leaned toward Bess Marvin, who sat next to her. They were both third graders in Mrs. Reynolds's class. Bess was one of Nancy's best friends.

"I wonder what's in the bag?" Nancy whispered to Bess.

"It looks like a lunch bag, so maybe it's food," Bess whispered back. She tossed her long blond hair over her shoulders

1

and glanced at Mrs. Reynolds. "Hmm. Or maybe not."

Nancy leaned forward in her seat. Mrs. Reynolds was pulling folded-up pieces of paper out of the bag.

"These have your names on them," Mrs. Reynolds explained. She let the pieces of paper flutter through her fingers and back into the bag. "For this project, we're going to need seven teams. I'm going to pick seven names out of this bag. Those students will be the team captains. Each captain will choose three or four other people to be on his or her team."

"If I'm a team captain, I'm not going to choose any girls," Jason Hutchings called out. He turned to his friend Mike Minelli, and they gave each other high fives.

"That's enough," Mrs. Reynolds said, frowning at the boys. "Anyway, each team will write a short story—a mystery short story set here at Carl Sandburg Elementary School. A week from tomorrow, all the teams will read their stories out loud in class, and we'll vote on the best one."

A mystery short story! Nancy sat up in

her seat. She loved mysteries. For one thing, she was the best detective at Carl Sandburg Elementary School. She had a special blue notebook that her father had given her. She wrote clues in it whenever she was working on a case.

Still, writing a mystery short story would be different from solving a mystery, Nancy thought—a different kind of fun. She was excited about trying it.

Across the room, George Fayne raised her hand. George was Bess's cousin and Nancy's other best friend. "Mrs. Reynolds? Won't it be kind of hard for all the team members to write together?" George asked.

"You'll take turns," Mrs. Reynolds explained with a smile. "You can decide on a story idea as a team. Then each team member will write one part of the story. The first person will write the first part. The second person will write the second part, and so on."

"Cool," George said. "Kind of like the baton relay." George, who was tall and had dark, curly hair, was really into sports.

Mrs. Reynolds reached into the paper

bag and picked out seven names for the team captains. "Katie Zaleski, Andrew Leoni, Julia Santos, Mari Cheng, Jason Hutchings, Nancy Drew . . . and Brenda Carlton," she read out loud.

"I knew I'd be one of the team captains," Brenda Carlton said smugly.

Bess glanced at Nancy and rolled her eyes. Nancy put her hand over her mouth to keep from giggling. Brenda wrote her own newspaper, which she printed on her father's computer. She always acted as if she was the most important person in the class.

Mrs. Reynolds had all the team captains take turns picking their teams. Nancy picked Bess, George, and Phoebe Archer. Brenda picked Jenny March, Emily Reeves, and her best friend, Alison Wegman. Jason Hutchings picked all boys, just as he'd said: Mike Minelli, Kyle Leddington, and Peter DeSands.

"I'm passing out the composition books you'll be using for your stories," Mrs. Reynolds said. She went up and down the aisles and gave each of the team leaders a shiny purple notebook. "Each person can

4

write his or her part and pass the notebook on to the next person on the team. Good luck!" she finished with a smile.

Nancy took one of the purple notebooks from Mrs. Reynolds. She opened the notebook to the first page. It was fresh and new and white—just waiting for a story to be written on it, Nancy thought eagerly.

"How about a story where all the third graders get kidnapped by aliens?" Phoebe suggested. She, Nancy, George, and Bess were in the lunchroom, eating lunch. They were trying to come up with ideas for their mystery.

"Aliens? Hmm. That might be too scary," Bess said. She picked up her fork and poked at the food on her plate. It was mushy and brown and gooey. "Speaking of scary . . . what *is* this, anyway? Yuck!"

"I think they took yesterday's mystery meat and put it in the blender or something," Nancy said, making a face.

Bess's eyes lit up. "That's it! 'The Mystery of the Mystery Meat.' That could be our story."

The other girls giggled. Bess started giggling, too. Pretty soon all four of them were laughing really hard.

"Okay, okay," George said, trying to sound serious. "We have to come up with more ideas. I know—what about a soccer mystery?"

"What kind of soccer mystery?" Nancy asked her.

George peeled a banana and took a big bite. "Maybe someone tries to keep our team from winning the big tournament," she said after a moment. "Or maybe someone steals all our balls and equipment and stuff."

"Computer viruses," Phoebe said suddenly. "What if there's a computer virus that takes over all the computers at the school? And then all the computers in River Heights. And then all the computers in the whole world!"

"That's a cool idea," Bess said. "I don't know anything about computer viruses, though. Do you?"

"Not really," Phoebe admitted, shaking her head. Nancy and George shook their heads, too.

Nancy took a forkful of mashed potatoes. She glanced around the lunchroom, searching for ideas. She saw the lunchroom lady taking money at the cash register. Kids were standing in line or walking around with trays. Others were eating, talking, and trading sandwiches.

Nancy saw Brenda, Alison, Jenny, and Emily sitting together. Jason Hutchings was sitting with Mike, Kyle, and Peter. They had their heads bent together. They're all working on their story ideas, she thought.

Nancy's gaze moved to the walls. On display were a bunch of collages made by the fifth graders. They had used objects like ice-cream sticks and bottle caps. Near them, over the doorway, was a banner that said Carl Sandburg Elementary School.

Carl Sandburg! Nancy thought. She turned to her friends. Her voice was high and excited as she spoke. "What if we do a mystery about Carl Sandburg?"

"You mean make up some guy named Carl Sandburg?" Phoebe said, looking puzzled.

"Carl Sandburg was a real person," Nancy explained. "He lived in Chicago, and he was a writer. My dad has a book of his poems and short stories at home." Chicago was close to River Heights, where Nancy and her friends lived.

"Is Carl Sandburg still alive?" George asked her.

"I don't think so," Nancy replied.

"I know, I know," Bess said, waving her hand in the air. "Oh, this is so cool. We could have the ghost of Carl Sandburg haunting the school."

"Yeah!" Phoebe said, grinning. "A ghost. I like that."

Nancy got a piece of paper out of her backpack, and the four of them began jotting down notes. Pretty soon they had a couple of ideas for how the story could go.

They also worked out a plan. Nancy would write the first part of the story. Bess would write the second part. George would write the third part, and Phoebe would write the ending.

"This is a totally cool idea for a story," Bess said. It was almost time to head out to the playground, for recess. "We'll definitely win the contest."

"Yeah, *right*. Dream on!"

Nancy and her friends glanced up. Brenda was standing there. She flipped her long, dark hair over her shoulder and smiled meanly at them.

"There's no way you're going to win the contest," Brenda went on. "Because *my* team is going to win. We're going to cream you guys!"

2
Top Secret!

You're going to cream us? Says who?"
Phoebe snapped at Brenda.

"Says me," Brenda snapped back. "First
of all, I'm the best writer in our class.
Second of all, we came up with an awesome idea for our story. It's going to blow
you guys out of the water."

Bess stood up and put her hands on her
hips. "Oh, yeah? I bet our idea is a million,
billion times better. It's about—"

"*Bess!*" George cried out, poking her
cousin in the arm. "Shhhh, you're not
supposed to tell!"

Bess's hands flew to her lips. "Oh, yeah. Oops."

"You are *not* the best writer in the class," Phoebe told Brenda huffily. "And your team isn't going to cream our team, because our team is going to cream your team instead!"

Brenda narrowed her eyes at Phoebe. "You want to bet?"

Phoebe looked startled. "Huh? Uh, sure."

Brenda smiled her mean smile again. "Okay, Phoebe. If my team wins, you have to sharpen my pencils for the rest of the year. If your team wins, I'll sharpen yours."

The rest of the year! That was a long time, Nancy thought.

Phoebe smiled uncertainly at Brenda. "Okay, uh, sure. You've got a bet."

"Great," Brenda said, turning to go. She glanced over her shoulder and added, "You'd better start practicing."

"Practicing what?" Phoebe asked her.

"Sharpening pencils," Brenda replied nastily.

That night after dinner, Nancy sat on the living room couch with her feet tucked under her. The purple notebook was propped on her lap, and she had a freshly sharpened pencil in her hand.

Her brown Labrador puppy, Choccolate Chip, was curled up in a ball next to her. Chip's eyes were closed, and she was snoring quietly. Once in a while Nancy would reach out to scratch Chip's ears. That made her tail thump rhythmically against the couch.

Carson Drew walked into the living room. "Here you go, Pudding Pie," he said, handing Nancy a fat book. "It's the collection of Carl Sandburg's poems and short stories you asked for. I got it at a used book store in Chicago years ago," he added.

"Thanks, Daddy," Nancy said eagerly.

She took the book from her father. The cover was old and worn. When she opened it, a pleasant dusty smell—an old-book smell—wafted up from the pages.

Carson sat down on the couch and pointed to the table of contents. "You might like the stories in this section. They're called 'Rootabaga Stories,' and

Carl Sandburg wrote them for children," he told her.

Nancy turned to the section with the "Rootabaga Stories." The stories had really great titles: "How Gimme the Ax Found Out About the Zigzag Railroad and Who Made It Zigzag" and "The Story of Jason Squiff and Why He Had a Popcorn Hat, Popcorn Mittens, and Popcorn Shoes."

"When Carl Sandburg wrote these stories, most stories for children had to do with kings and queens and castles," Carson explained. "He wanted to do something . . . well, a little different."

"I know!" Nancy said suddenly. "I could use some of Carl Sandburg's titles and characters in *our* story! You know, maybe as clues or something."

Carson patted her on the shoulder. "That's a terrific idea, Pudding Pie. See, you're a brilliant writer as well as a brilliant detective." His eyes twinkled as he rose. "I'll leave you to do your work now. Writers need lots of peace and quiet to create their masterpieces, you know."

"Okay, Daddy," Nancy said with a grin.

Carson went into his study to do some work of his own. He was a lawyer and was in the middle of a big new case.

Nancy turned her attention back to the "Rootabaga Stories" and read a couple of them. She really loved Sandburg's funny titles and characters, and his funny style of writing, too.

After a while she had lots of great ideas swirling around in her head. She was ready to begin writing.

Picking up her pencil, she wrote:

THE GHOST OF CARL SANDBURG ELEMENTARY SCHOOL

by Nancy Drew, Bess Marvin,
George Fayne, and Phoebe Archer

Once upon a time, there was a school called the Carl Sandburg Elementary School. It was a really nice school, and everyone liked it there.

That is, until the ghost started haunting it.

At first, no one believed there *was* a ghost. After all, ghosts don't really exist, right? But then everyone *had* to believe it because of the weird stuff that started happening.

One morning one of the kids found this note taped to his cubby:

A TIN BRASS GOOSE
TWO BLUE RATS
THREE WHISPERING CATS

It was written in creepy-looking red ink that looked like blood. Or maybe it *was* blood. The teachers and the principal figured one of the kids had written it. The principal said during the morning announcements that the person who wrote it should come forward right away. But no one did.

And then someone found the *second* note. . . .

Just then Chocolate Chip stirred, opened her eyes, and let out a big doggie yawn. Nancy yawned, too. It was very late.

"Let's go up to bed, Chip," Nancy said,

closing the purple notebook. "I think we've done enough work for one night."

The next morning in school, Nancy walked into her classroom. The purple notebook was in her backpack. Mrs. Reynolds hadn't arrived yet, but most of the kids were at their desks. They all seemed to be talking about the short-story contest.

"We've got the coolest idea for a mystery!" Katie Zaleski was saying in a loud, excited voice. Katie was one of the team captains. She got excited about lots of stuff.

"Ours is way cooler," Brenda said. She shot a smug look at Phoebe and then at Nancy.

Emily Reeves, who was on Brenda's team, added, "But it's top secret. We're not telling anyone what it is."

"Well, ours is top secret, too," Katie said quickly.

As Nancy passed Kyle's desk, she overheard him say to Peter in a low voice, "Oh, great. We don't even have an idea for our story yet."

Nancy reached her desk and sat down.

As she slid her backpack off her shoulders, Bess leaned toward her and whispered, "Did you write the beginning of . . . um . . . *you-know-what* last night?" she whispered.

"Uh-huh," Nancy said. She reached into her backpack and pulled out the purple notebook.

She held it across the aisle to Bess. "Your turn," she said.

Just then a pair of hands reached out and grabbed the notebook from her. Nancy whirled around. Mike Minelli was standing in the aisle. He had the notebook, and he was opening it to the first page.

"Give that back!" Nancy cried out.

Ignoring her, Mike took a few steps back. Everyone in the class had fallen silent.

In a loud voice, Mike began to read: "'Once upon a time, there was a school called the Carl Sandburg Elementary School. It was a really nice school, and everyone liked it there. That is, until—'"

3
Gone!

No!" Bess leaped out of her chair and swiped the purple notebook out of Mike's hands.

With a nasty laugh, Mike grabbed for the notebook again, but Bess was too fast for him. She went back to her desk, shoved the notebook in her backpack, and hugged the backpack to her chest. She glared furiously at Mike.

"Way to go, Bess!" George called out from across the room.

"That was really mean," Nancy told Mike angrily. "Our story is private and top secret, like everyone else's."

"I guess it's not so private and top secret anymore," Mike said with a grin.

Mrs. Reynolds came into the room just then. Mike scooted quickly into his seat with a noisy scraping of his chair.

"Good morning, class," Mrs. Reynolds said. She set her books down on her desk. "This morning we're going to be doing language arts."

Mrs. Reynolds picked up a piece of chalk and began writing on the chalkboard. Nancy turned to stare at Mike. What had he meant by saying that Nancy's team's story wasn't so private and top secret anymore? He'd read only the first couple of lines out loud.

Or had he managed to sneak a peek at more than that?

Over the weekend Bess and George wrote their parts of the story. On Monday after school, the two of them, Nancy, and Phoebe met at Nancy's house to go over the story so far.

The four girls were sitting cross-legged on Nancy's bed. Nancy had just read her part of the story, and now Bess was about to read hers. She had the purple notebook propped in her lap.

"Wait till you guys hear what I wrote," Bess said, flipping through the pages. "It is *so* awesome."

"Speaking of awesome, how about a snack?"

Nancy glanced up to see Hannah Gruen walk into the room, carrying a tray. Hannah was the Drews' housekeeper. She had been with them since Nancy's mother died five years earlier.

Hannah set the tray down on the nightstand. There was a big bowl of buttered popcorn, four glasses of apple juice, and lots of napkins. Chocolate Chip, who'd been asleep on the floor, woke up and sniffed at the popcorn.

"Thanks, Hannah!" the girls said in unison.

"You mystery writers need your energy," Hannah said, winking. "Let me know if you want refills on the juice."

After Hannah left the room, Bess grabbed a fistful of popcorn and stuffed it into her mouth. A piece tumbled to the floor. Chip promptly scarfed it up. The other girls started in on the popcorn, too.

"Mmm, yummy," Bess said. "Okay. So, here's my part of the story. Are you guys ready?"

"Ready," Phoebe said, nodding. Nancy and George nodded, too.

Bess took a sip of her apple juice. Then she began to read in a dramatic-sounding voice:

The person who found the second note was a really cute girl named Tess. Tess had awesome taste in clothes. In fact, she was wearing a really cute pink T-shirt that day and these cool jeans with daisy patches.

Anyway, Tess found the note taped to her cubby. It was written in creepy-looking red ink, just like the first one. It said:

FOUR MOONS
FIVE RUSTY RATS
SIX GIRLS WITH BALLOONS

Tess was really freaked out by the note. She screamed at the top of her

lungs. A bunch of kids came running up to her and asked her what was going on. (Some of them asked her where she got her T-shirt. She told them at Girl Power, at the mall.)

Bess closed the notebook and looked up with a big, wide smile. "Well?"

"It's very *you*, Bess," Phoebe said, giggling.

"It's really good," Nancy added, grabbing some more popcorn. "Okay, George, your turn."

George reached over and took the notebook from Bess. She opened it to her page, cleared her throat, and began to read:

What did the notes mean? No one could figure them out. And then one day this girl named Gerry was walking down the hall after soccer practice. She was going over some key moves in her mind because there was a big game coming up. Anyway, she was turning the corner and thinking about headers when she saw *it*.

She saw the *ghost!*

Right away Gerry stopped thinking about soccer. She tried her hardest not to scream.

The ghost was an old man with white hair and glasses. He was wearing a suit with a vest and a bow tie. Gerry knew he was a ghost and not a real person because his skin was kind of silvery white, like a ghost's.

Gerry stopped and stared at him. He stopped and stared at her. Gerry wondered if she should do a header on him, to scare him away.

Then the ghost opened his ghostly mouth. In a low, ghostly voice he said: "The fog comes on little cat feet." It sounded like some sort of poem.

Then the ghost disappeared.

"Wow, that's really spooky!" Bess exclaimed, hugging a pillow to her chest.

"I got goose bumps," Nancy said. "See?" She raised her arms, to show everyone.

"What's that stuff about 'little cat feet'?" Phoebe asked George.

"It's from one of Carl Sandburg's poems. That was Nancy's idea," George replied. Then she handed the purple notebook to Phoebe.

"Your turn," George said with a grin. "You've got a really important part to write. The ending!"

"Make it super-cool, okay?" Bess said to Phoebe.

Phoebe took the notebook and shrugged. "Uh, okay. No problem. I'll have it by tomorrow."

Tuesday was a cloudy day. The sky was gray, and it looked as though it might rain.

During recess Nancy, Bess, and George were swinging on the swings. Nancy liked to pump her legs really hard and make the swing go way up high. So did George. Bess liked to make the swing wobble from side to side, in figure eights.

"Three more days until our stories are due," George said as she rose in the air. "We're way ahead of schedule."

"I bet we're going to win first prize," Bess said, wobbling from side to side. "I have a good feeling about it."

Nancy tipped her head back for a second so she could look up at the sky. The gray-white clouds flashed and blurred in her vision. When she looked back down, she saw Phoebe racing across the playground toward them.

Nancy dragged her feet on the ground and tugged on her swing to make it slow down. "Hi, Phoebe!" she called out.

Then Nancy noticed that Phoebe seemed really upset. "What's wrong?" she asked.

Phoebe skidded to a halt in front of the swing set. "It's the purple notebook!" she cried. "It's gone!"

4

A Real Mystery

What do you mean the notebook is gone?" Nancy exclaimed.

Bess and George brought their swings to a stop, too. "It's gone?" Bess repeated.

"I wrote the ending last night, just like I said I would," Phoebe said in a shaky voice. "And I put the purple notebook in my backpack this morning. We were going to get together at the Double Dip later so I could read you guys what I wrote. Remember?"

"We remember," Bess said, nodding. "I was going to try that new Triple Toffee

29

Taste Explosion Sundae, with extra cherries on top, and—"

"Bess, let Phoebe talk!" George interrupted.

"Right after lunch, I was on my way out here," Phoebe went on. "I stopped for a minute to put my hair clips in my backpack because they kept falling out. You know, the yellow butterfly ones I got at the mall? Anyway, when I opened the backpack, I noticed that the purple notebook wasn't there."

Nancy thought for a minute. "When was the last time you saw it?"

"Right before lunch, while Mrs. Reynolds was making us do those math tables," Phoebe replied. "I opened my backpack to get a pencil out, and I saw the notebook there."

"Maybe you left the notebook in class," Bess suggested hopefully.

Phoebe shook her head. "I don't think so. I never took it out."

"Did you have your backpack with you the whole time between then and now?" George asked her.

Phoebe frowned. "Yes. I mean, no. I was

at my cubby right before lunch. Emily was across the hall, and she told me she wanted to talk to me about something. I left my backpack in the cubby while I was talking to her."

Phoebe's lower lip began to tremble. She looked as though she was about to cry. "I spent a really long time last night writing a super-cool ending," she said miserably. "And now it's gone! The whole story is gone!"

Nancy got off the swing. "We'll find the notebook," she said with determination. "Phoebe, you come with me. Bess and George, here's what you should do."

For the next half hour, the four girls searched for the purple notebook. Nancy and Phoebe retraced Phoebe's path from Mrs. Reynolds's classroom to her cubby to the playground. Bess and George looked in the lunchroom and the bathroom and the trashcans. But the notebook was nowhere to be found.

When they met up again just outside of their classroom, Phoebe said, "What could have happened to the notebook? It's all my fault!" She looked really upset.

"There are only two things that could have happened to it," Nancy pointed out. "Either you lost it, or . . ." Her voice trailed off.

"Or someone stole it," Bess finished.

"Yeah. And if someone stole it, we'll have to find the thief," Nancy said. "Our mystery short story is turning into a *real* mystery!"

"Let's write down the clues we have so far," Nancy suggested.

It was almost five o'clock, and she and George were sitting in the Drews' backyard. They'd just finished soccer practice, so they still had their soccer clothes on.

The late afternoon sun peeked out from behind a bunch of clouds as the two girls leaned back in their lawn chairs and sipped lemonade. Nearby, Chocolate Chip was lying in the grass, busily gnawing on an old rubber bone. From the kitchen window came the sounds of Hannah preparing dinner.

Nancy had a notebook spread out on her lap. It wasn't the purple notebook, but her special blue detective notebook.

33

Her father had given it to her to write clues and suspects in, for when she was solving mysteries.

George stretched her long legs out in front of her. "Hmm, clues," she said thoughtfully. "Clues," she repeated. She glanced at Nancy and wrinkled her nose. "Uh, do we *have* any clues?"

"I guess not," Nancy said. "But we *do* know some stuff. We know that the purple notebook was definitely in Phoebe's backpack this morning in class . . ."

". . . so it disappeared sometime between before lunch and right after lunch, when she put her hair clips in her backpack," George added.

"And the only time she left her backpack alone was right before lunch, when she was hanging out at her cubby—*yuck!*" Nancy cried out.

Chocolate Chip had bounded up and deposited the rubber bone in Nancy's lap. It was all wet and drooly.

Making a face, Nancy picked up the chew toy gingerly. Then she threw it to the far end of the yard. Chip barked and went bounding after it.

"Phoebe left the backpack in her cubby for a minute because Emily said she wanted to talk to her about something," George reminded Nancy.

Nancy nodded. She opened her blue notebook to a clean page, picked up a pen, and wrote "Emily Reeves."

Nancy chewed on the end of her pen. "Emily is on Brenda's team," she said slowly.

George sat up in her lawn chair. "Oh, yeah, that's right."

"And Brenda really wants to win the short-story contest," Nancy went on.

George's eyes lit up. "Brenda and Emily must have teamed up to steal our story — and maybe Jenny and Alison, too!"

5

Copycats and Copyrats

But why would Brenda and her teammates want to steal your story?" Carson asked Nancy.

It was Wednesday morning, and the two of them were having breakfast.

Nancy spooned some blueberry granola into her mouth. "I'm not totally sure they did, Daddy," she said. "But Brenda has this bet going with Phoebe. If Brenda's team wins, Phoebe has to sharpen Brenda's pencils—for the rest of the year!"

"That's quite a bet," Carson remarked, raising his mug of coffee to his lips.

"Plus, Brenda always likes to win, any-

36

way," Nancy went on. "Plus, the only time Phoebe left her backpack alone was when Emily called her over to talk."

"What if Emily really *did* call Phoebe over just to talk? And maybe someone else who's not even on Brenda's team took the opportunity to steal the purple notebook?" Carson pointed out.

Nancy considered this. "That's true, Daddy. I hadn't thought of that. I guess I'd better talk to Emily." She grinned. "You're a pretty awesome detective."

Carson laughed. "Detective's *assistant* is more like it, Pudding Pie."

Nancy found Emily right before class, at her cubby. Emily was rummaging through her backpack, as though she was looking for something. Kids were starting to head into Mrs. Reynolds's classroom.

Nancy hung back for a second, watching. Emily pulled out a bunch of marking pens, then a pink hair ribbon, then a paperback book with a ripped-looking cover. Nancy wasn't sure, but she thought that the title of it was *The Monster That Ate New York*.

Emily stuffed the markers, then the ribbon, then the book back into her backpack. Then she pulled out two purple notebooks.

Two purple notebooks? Nancy did a double take. But Emily had moved a little, so her body was blocking Nancy's view. Nancy couldn't see what she was holding in her hands.

Without wasting another second, Nancy rushed up to her. "Hey, Emily!" she called out.

Emily whirled around. Her eyes widened. Nancy wondered, Was it her imagination, or did Emily seem kind of nervous?

Emily hugged her backpack to her chest. Nancy couldn't see the purple notebooks. "Uh, hi, Nancy," Emily said. "W-what do you want?"

"I wanted to talk to you about the short-story contest," Nancy said with a friendly smile. "See—"

But before she had a chance to finish, Emily said, "Uh, I can't talk right now, okay?" With that, she turned and headed into the classroom.

Nancy frowned. What was going on? Emily was definitely acting weird about *something*.

Just then Phoebe and Bess came up to her. "Hi, Nancy!" Bess called out. "Phoebe and I have been doing some detective work. Okay, so, what if there are alien life-forms here at Carl Sandburg Elementary School, and they stole our purple notebook to take back to their mother ship?"

Nancy giggled. Bess giggled, too. Phoebe cracked a smile, but her eyes were troubled. Nancy figured that she still felt bad about the notebook being missing.

"Listen," Nancy said, trying to be serious. "I have a different theory." She filled Phoebe and Bess in on what she and George had discussed the day before. She added the stuff about Emily acting weird just a few minutes ago.

"So you think Emily and Brenda and maybe those other girls on their team stole our story?" Bess said when Nancy had finished.

Before Nancy had a chance to reply,

Phoebe exclaimed, "I bet that's what happened! Nancy, you've solved the mystery!"

"Well, I don't know about that," Nancy said. "We still have to—"

Just at that moment, Brenda passed by them. "Hey," she called out, tossing her dark hair over her shoulders. "How's your *loser story* coming along?"

Bess marched right up to Brenda. "Why don't *you* tell *us*, Brenda?" she snapped.

Brenda frowned. She looked totally confused. "Huh? What are you talking about, Bess?"

Nancy ran up to Bess and poked her in the arm. She didn't want to accuse Brenda—or anyone on Brenda's team—without any proof. "Listen," she said, smiling at Brenda. "Our, um, purple notebook is missing. You haven't seen it, have you?"

Brenda's dark eyes flashed. "Your purple notebook? You mean, the one with your story in it?" She began to laugh. "Wow, that was really dumb of you guys to lose it. Now you're *definitely* going to lose the contest!"

With that, she marched into the classroom.

"She is soooooo mean," Bess said through clenched teeth.

"I think she's totally lying," Phoebe said quickly. "Don't you think she was lying, Nancy?"

"I'm not sure. Maybe." Nancy added, "We'd better get to class. The bell's about to ring."

"Today we're going to start with a spelling review," Mrs. Reynolds announced. "Jason, can you come up to the board and spell *pancake?*"

Groaning, Jason went to the front of the room. Nancy picked up her pen and began to write *pancake* herself, in her spelling book. She had gotten as far as *P-A-N-* when a folded-up piece of paper landed on her desk with a quiet *thunk*.

Startled, she glanced up. Bess was staring at her and wriggling her eyebrows.

"Is this from you?" Nancy whispered.

"From George," Bess whispered back. Nancy peered across the room. George was staring at her and wriggling her eyebrows, too_ She pointed to the note that Nancy was now holding in her hand.

Curious, Nancy put the note in her lap. She opened it carefully, so the paper wouldn't make a rustling noise.

George had written:

I think I know who stole our story. And it's not who we were talking about yesterday. We have to talk right away!

"Nancy Drew!"

Nancy glanced up, startled. Mrs. Reynolds was frowning at her.

"I called your name three times," Mrs. Reynolds told her.

Nancy quickly refolded the note in her lap. She hoped that Mrs. Reynolds wouldn't see. "I'm sorry," she apologized.

Mrs. Reynolds held up a piece of chalk. "Would you come up here and spell the word *pioneer* for us, please?"

Nancy slipped George's note into the pocket of her jeans, rose from her chair, and started down the aisle. She heard the sound of snickering and turned around. It

43

was Brenda. Brenda always loved to see other kids get into trouble, especially Nancy.

Trying to ignore her, Nancy took the chalk from Mrs. Reynolds and began to write on the chalkboard. As she wrote, she wondered about George's note. What new information did she have? Who else besides Brenda, Emily, and their team members could have stolen "The Ghost of Carl Sandburg Elementary School"?

The rest of the morning seemed to drag on forever. As soon as the bell rang for lunch, Nancy hurried over to George's desk. "Well?" she demanded.

Bess and Phoebe gathered around George's desk, too. "What's going on?" Bess said.

George's eyes were shining. "Okay, guys, listen to this," she said. "When I was walking into class this morning, I passed Jason and Mike." She glanced around to make sure they weren't listening. "They were talking about how they finally came up with a cool story idea yesterday. And

44

that they're definitely going to win the contest!"

Nancy frowned. "Yesterday? Like, the same day our notebook disappeared?"

George nodded her head briskly, which made her brown curls bounce. "Exactly. And there's more. I heard Mike say something about cats and rats."

"Cats and rats—just like in *our* story!" Bess exclaimed. "'A tin brass goose, two blue rats, three whispering cats . . .'"

"Huh?" Phoebe said, looking puzzled.

"Don't you get it?" George said excitedly. "I think Jason and Mike and the guys stole our story so they could copy it and pretend it was theirs!"

6

Starting from Scratch

I don't know," Nancy said doubtfully. "There's no way the boys could get away with stealing our story. I mean, if they read our story on Friday and pretend it's theirs, we'd tell Mrs. Reynolds."

"How could we prove it was our story, though?" George pointed out. "It would be the boys' word against ours."

"That's true," Nancy admitted.

"I know!" Bess said, bouncing up and down. "Why don't we get one of the boys to tell us what their story's about?"

"Oh, yeah, right," Phoebe said, rolling her eyes.

"No, no, I mean it. I think I have a way." Bess grinned and started walking toward the lunchroom. "Come on, guys. Just let me do all the talking, okay?"

The girls stood in line and got their lunch trays. Today lunch was chicken nuggets, peas, and fruit cocktail.

George glanced around. "Hey, where's Phoebe?"

"She had to go to the bathroom," Bess said. She scoped out the lunchroom. "Great, there's Peter and Kyle! Come on, follow me."

Bess made a beeline for the boys' table. Nancy and George trailed after her. They found Peter and Kyle making sculptures out of the chicken nuggets and peas.

"Doomsday Tower!" Peter said loudly. He made a tall stack of chicken nuggets on his plate.

"Beware, for the evil warrior comes to attack the tower!" Kyle replied. He tossed peas at the stack of chicken nuggets. Then he caught sight of Bess, Nancy, and George and began throwing peas at them, instead. "Intruder alert! Intruder alert!"

"Stop that!" Bess exclaimed.

Kyle laughed, but he stopped the pea attack.

"What do you want?" Peter asked them, munching on a chicken nugget.

Nancy started to open her mouth, then clamped it shut. She remembered what Bess had said about wanting to do all the talking.

Bess smoothed her hair behind her ears and smiled her best fake-friendly smile. "We just wanted to tell you that your team's story idea sounds really, really cool. I bet you'll definitely win first place."

Peter and Kyle stared at each other. "Huh?" Peter said after a moment. "How did you hear about our story?"

"Yeah, how?" Kyle echoed. He looked pretty suspicious.

"Oh, you know," Bess said vaguely. "Stuff gets around. Anyway, I really wish *we'd* thought about doing a story about, um, killer bees attacking our school."

Kyle made a face. "Killer bees? No way! Our story's about a mad scientist and a—"

Peter hurled a chicken nugget at Kyle. It bounced off Kyle's nose and landed on the table. "Shut up, Leddington! We're not supposed to talk about it!"

"Oh, yeah," Kyle said sheepishly. "Sorry."

Bess shot a triumphant look at Nancy and George. Then she turned to the boys and said, "Our chicken nuggets are getting cold. Bye!"

The three girls found an empty table nearby and sat down. Seconds later Phoebe joined them. She set her tray down and said, a little breathlessly, "So? What did I miss?"

Nancy filled her in on their conversation with Peter and Kyle. She also remembered to update George on her earlier conversation with Emily, at Emily's cubby.

"So now we have *two* suspects: Brenda's team and Jason's team," Bess said, popping a chicken nugget into her mouth. "By the way, wasn't it totally, totally brilliant how I got Kyle and Peter to confess everything?"

"Uh, Bess? All Kyle said was that their

story had a mad scientist in it," Nancy pointed out. "And *our* story doesn't."

"That's true," Bess said, frowning.

George took a sip of her milk. "Maybe the boys just added that, to make their story a little different from ours."

"That's true, too," Bess said.

Pushing her tray aside, Nancy pulled her blue detective notebook out of her backpack and opened it up to the page with the words *Emily Reeves* on it. Uncapping a blue marking pen, she crossed out Emily's name and wrote:

SUSPECTS
<u>Brenda's team</u>

∗Brenda really, really wants to win the contest!

∗Emily called Phoebe over to talk to her on Tuesday, right before lunch. That's the only time Phoebe left her backpack alone. And the purple notebook was gone right after that. So maybe someone else on Brenda's team stole it while Emily and Phoebe were talking?

∗Emily had two purple notebooks

today. Plus, she was acting kind of nervous and weird.

<u>Jason Hutchings's team</u>
*Jason and the boys just came up with their story idea on Tuesday—the same day our notebook disappeared.
*George heard Jason and Mike talking about how their story has cats and rats in it, just like ours.

Nancy chewed on the end of her pen. After a moment she said, "Hey, you know what? What if we don't find our story thief by Friday? We should really start trying to rewrite our story, from memory."

"You mean start from scratch?" Phoebe said in surprise. "But won't Mrs. Reynolds understand if we don't turn in a story for the contest? I mean, someone stole our notebook!"

"We should try, anyway," George said. "We did have a really awesome story." She added, "I think I remember *my* part."

"I think I remember most of *my* part, too," Bess chimed in. "It was about that really cute girl, Tess, and her really cute clothes."

The girls spent the rest of the lunch period trying to re-create "The Ghost of Carl Sandburg Elementary School." They didn't try to re-create it word for word. Instead, Nancy, then Bess, then George, then Phoebe tried to remember the key points in each of their parts. Bess took notes, scribbling furiously in a small notepad with smiley faces all over it.

When it was her turn, Phoebe hesitated. "Okay, so then, the girl named Gerry has this, um, note . . ." she said slowly.

"The note about the fog and the little cat feet," George prompted her.

Phoebe nodded. "Right! And then Gerry takes the note, and, um—" Phoebe was interrupted by the recess bell. She scooped her tray up and rose quickly to her feet. "Come on, let's go on the swings for a while," she said brightly. "Maybe that'll help me remember."

The four girls emptied their trays in the trash and stacked them on the shelf. They headed into the hallway, chatting about their story.

Lots of other kids were in the hallway, walking toward the schoolyard. Everyone was talking and laughing and making a lot of noise.

Just then Nancy and her friends heard a piercing scream.

7

A Creepy Note

What was *that?*" Bess cried out.

Nancy started running in the direction of the scream. It sounded as if it had come from somewhere near their classroom.

When she and the other girls reached that part of the building, they found a small crowd of kids and hall monitors gathered around the third graders' cubbies. Katie Zaleski was standing at her cubby, looking as pale as a ghost.

Nancy squeezed through the crowd and rushed up to Katie. "What's going on?" she asked her breathlessly.

"Look!" Katie pointed to something

that was taped to her cubby. It was a note written in drippy red ink that looked like blood. The note said:

A TIN BRASS GOOSE
TWO BLUE RATS
THREE WHISPERING CATS

Nancy gasped. That was from their story! The red ink was from their story, too!

Mrs. Reynolds broke through the crowd. "Exactly what is going on here?" she demanded. "Who screamed?"

"S-someone t-taped that to my c-cubby," Katie stammered, pointing to the note.

Mrs. Reynolds pulled the note off the cubby and studied it. She glanced at the dozen or so faces that were gathered around. "Does anyone know anything about this?"

Nancy gulped. Bess, George, and Phoebe were all staring at her with wide eyes. Nancy wondered: Should they tell Mrs. Reynolds about their story and about the missing purple notebook?

Before Nancy had a chance to say anything, Mrs. Reynolds said, "I'm sure this is someone's idea of a practical joke. I don't want to see it happening again." She crumpled up the note.

Nancy glanced over at Brenda and Emily, who were standing in the back of the crowd. Brenda was scribbling like mad in a little notepad. What was *that* about? Was she planning to write an article about the note for the *Carlton News?*

Emily glanced at Nancy, and then glanced away. Nancy wondered if she knew something. Jason, Mike, Kyle, and Peter were nowhere to be seen.

Nancy was now one hundred percent sure that her team's purple notebook wasn't just missing or lost. Someone had definitely stolen it.

And now someone—or a bunch of someones—were turning "The Ghost of Carl Sandburg Elementary School" into reality!

"I knew this Triple Toffee Taste Explosion Sundae would be totally awesome!" Bess exclaimed. She took an extra-big spoonful of whipped cream and stuffed it into her mouth. "Yum! You guys want to try some?"

Bess, George, and Nancy were hanging out at the Double Dip, their favorite ice-cream parlor. They had gotten permission from their parents to go there after school. Phoebe wasn't with them, because she had gone shopping with her mom.

"No, thanks, Bess," George said. "I'm happy with my High-Protein Blueberry-Granola-Nut Milkshake."

"And I'm getting really stuffed on my Killer Chocolate Parfait," Nancy said.

She pulled her blue detective notebook out of her backpack and opened it up to the page about their missing-story mystery. "So. Who do you think put that note on Katie's cubby?" she said, uncapping her purple pen.

"Brenda and her creepy teammates," Bess said immediately.

"Jason and *his* creepy teammates," George said, almost at the same time.

"But what if maybe it was someone else? Someone we haven't even thought of?" Nancy tapped her pen on the table, trying to sort it all out.

After a moment she said, "Maybe someone decided to steal our story and act out parts of it, make them become real. You know, as a prank or something."

"Yeah, but who?" Bess mumbled, popping a cherry into her mouth.

Nancy sighed. "I'm not sure."

Just then Jenny and Emily walked into the Double Dip.

"Hey," Jenny called out as she and Emily passed the girls' table. Emily said nothing.

"Hey," Nancy, George, and Bess replied, in unison.

Emily went ahead to find an empty table. Jenny paused and stared at Bess's sundae. "What's that? It looks really gross," she said, making a face.

"It's a Triple Toffee Taste Explosion Sundae, and it's totally *not* gross. It just looks that way because I kind of mixed the caramel syrup up with the ice cream and the crunchy toffee bits and the— Anyway, you want to try some?" Bess offered.

"Uh, no, thanks," Jenny said, shaking her head.

"How's your story coming?" George

asked Jenny with an innocent expression.

Jenny shrugged. "Well, uh . . . okay, I guess. We kind of fell behind, but I guess we're kind of catching up now, and—"

Overhearing, Emily rushed up to Jenny and glared at her icily. "We're not supposed to talk about our story with these—with *anybody*. Remember?"

"Oh, yeah," Jenny murmured.

Nancy glanced at Emily and smiled. "I keep meaning to ask you. Yesterday before lunch you were hanging out at your cubby, right? And you wanted to talk to Phoebe about something."

Emily looked confused. "Huh? I didn't talk to Phoebe yesterday before lunch."

"Are you sure?" Nancy asked her.

"Positive," Emily said. "I walked to the lunchroom with Jennie and Alison, straight from class. I didn't even stop at my cubby." She turned to Jenny. "Okay, I'm totally starving. Can we go order now?"

When Emily and Jenny had gone, Nancy turned to her friends. "George! Bess! I think I know who stole our purple notebook!" she announced.

8

And the Winner Is . . .

Bess's mouth dropped open. "You mean Emily's the one?" she said.

Nancy shook her head. "Nope."

"Jenny?" George guessed.

Nancy shook her head again. "Nope. Listen, I'm not going to tell you guys right now, okay? I have a plan. Besides, I want to make sure I'm right."

Usually when Nancy was close to solving a case, she got really excited. This time, though, was different because the new person she suspected of taking the notebook was the last person she would have suspected.

62

Bess's voice broke into her thoughts. "You have a plan, Nancy? What is it? Tell us while I finish my sundae—it's melting."

"George, you're stepping on my foot! *Ow!*" Bess whispered.

"Sorry!" George whispered back.

"Shh, someone's going to hear us," Nancy whispered to both of them.

The three girls were scrunched together in the shadowy doorway of Mrs. Reynolds's classroom. They were in a good position to see the third graders' cubbies.

It was Thursday, and all the other kids were in the lunchroom. Nancy and her friends had gotten hall passes to go to the bathroom, so they didn't have much time.

"Why are we doing this again?" Bess asked Nancy.

"We're catching the notebook thief," Nancy replied. "Shh!"

They stood in total silence for the next few minutes. Nancy fidgeted uncomfortably. It was hard to stay still. She could feel Bess and George fidgeting, too.

After a while they heard footsteps coming down the hall. Actually, it was more like the sound of rubber soles squeaking on the linoleum floor. Nancy motioned for the girls to step back, and held her breath.

The squeaking stopped. Nancy listened very carefully. She heard the sound of paper rustling, and then a small ripping sound. It was like the sound of tape being ripped from a tape dispenser.

Nancy gave Bess and George a signal. All at once, the three girls popped out of their hiding place.

"Phoebe!" Bess cried out.

Phoebe was standing at one of the cubbies. She had a note in her hand, written in drippy red ink. She was just about to tape it to the cubby.

Seeing Nancy and her friends, Phoebe gasped and dropped the note to the floor. Nancy picked it up.

It said:

FOUR MOONS
FIVE RUSTY RATS
SIX GIRLS WITH BALLOONS

"I don't get it," George said, looking confused. "Does this mean you stole our purple notebook? Pretended to steal it, I mean?"

Phoebe hung her head. "Yes," she whispered.

"Why, Phoebe?" Nancy asked her.

"I'm really sorry," Phoebe said in a quiet voice. "See, when I got the notebook on Monday, and it was my turn to write my part, I kind of, um . . . I just couldn't seem to write it. No matter how hard I tried, the words just wouldn't come out."

"I think that's called writer's blocks," Bess offered.

"Writer's *block*," George corrected.

"Yeah, that," Phoebe said, nodding. "Anyway, I didn't want to let you guys down. And I didn't want to lose my bet to that creep Brenda. So I decided I'd pretend that the notebook got stolen."

"Why were you doing this stuff with the notes?" Nancy asked her.

Phoebe shrugged. "I don't know. Just to make things more confusing. I figured, if you guys had enough suspects and clues and weird stuff happening, you'd never suspect me."

She added, "Plus, Mrs. Reynolds would probably get so mad about the notes that she'd cancel the whole short-story contest or something. That way I definitely wouldn't lose my bet to Brenda, because the bet would be off."

George turned to Nancy. "How did you know? That it was Phoebe, I mean."

"Emily told us that she never talked to Phoebe at her cubby yesterday," Nancy explained to George and Bess.

"Oh, yeah," Phoebe said, shaking her head. "I made up that story about Emily to make her and her teammates look guilty. I guess that was a dumb lie to tell." She looked at the girls, her eyes shiny with tears. "I'm really sorry about everything. I should have just told you guys the truth, from the beginning."

"Yeah, you should have," Bess told her, pouting angrily.

"You really let us down," Nancy added.

George nodded in agreement.

"I'm really, really sorry," Phoebe said again.

She looked so upset that Nancy felt sorry for her. "You really *should* have told us the truth from the beginning," Nancy said. "We could have helped you with your ending." She glanced at George and Bess and added, "I guess we still could."

George shrugged. "Yeah, okay."

Bess shrugged, too. "We *are* a team." She stopped pouting and smiled a little at Phoebe.

On Friday, the day the stories were due, Nancy got up in front of the class to read her team's story. Her team was going first, and she had butterflies in her stomach. She looked at all the faces of her classmates, took a deep breath, and began reading:

"Once upon a time, there was a school called Carl Sandburg Elementary School. It was a really nice school, and everyone liked it there.

"That is, until the ghost started haunting it.

"At first no one believed there *was* a ghost. After all, ghosts don't really exist, right? But then everyone *had* to believe it because of the weird stuff that started happening.

"One morning one of the kids found this note taped to his cubby:

"A TIN BRASS GOOSE
TWO BLUE RATS
THREE WHISPERING CATS

"It was written in creepy-looking red ink that looked like blood. Or maybe it *was* blood. The teachers and the principal figured one of the kids had written it. The principal said during the morning announcements that the person who wrote it should come forward right away. But no one did.

"And then someone found the *second* note.

"The person who found the second note was a really cute girl named Tess. Tess had awesome taste in clothes. In fact, she was wearing a really cute pink T-shirt that day, and these cool jeans with daisy patches.

"Anyway, Tess found the note taped to her cubby. It was written in creepy-looking red ink, just like the first one. It said:

"FOUR MOONS
FIVE RUSTY RATS
SIX GIRLS WITH BALLOONS

"Tess was really freaked out by the note. She screamed at the top of her lungs. A bunch of kids came running up to her and asked her what was going on. (Some of them asked her where she got her T-shirt. She told them at Girl Power, at the mall.)

"What did the notes mean? No one could figure them out. And then one day this girl named Gerry was walking down the hall after soccer practice. She was going over some key moves in her mind because there was a big game coming up.

"Anyway, she was turning the corner and thinking about headers when she saw *it*.

"She saw *the ghost!*

"Right away Gerry stopped thinking about soccer. She tried her hardest not to scream.

"The ghost was an old man with white hair and glasses. He was wearing a suit with a vest and a bow tie. Gerry knew he was a ghost and not a real person because his skin was kind of silvery white, like a ghost's.

"Gerry stopped and stared at him. He stopped and stared at her. Gerry wondered if she should do a header on him, to scare him away.

"Then the ghost opened his ghostly mouth. In a low, ghostly voice he said: 'The fog comes on little cat feet.' It sounded like some sort of poem.

"Then the ghost disappeared.

"Gerry was really freaked out. But she decided that maybe if she and Tess teamed up, they could solve the mystery of the ghost.

"Gerry and Tess came up with a plan. One day, after school, they waited in the place where Gerry had seen the ghost. They hid in a doorway and waited, and waited.

"After a while, the ghost appeared! Tess started to scream, but Gerry kicked her, so Tess shut up.

"The ghost looked right and left. He had another one of those bloody-looking notes. He was about to tape it to one of the kids' cubbies."'One, two, three,' Gerry whispered. 'Go!'

"She and Tess jumped out from their hiding place and yelled: 'Boo!'

"The ghost screamed. 'Oh, my, you surprised me,' he said.

"His voice was so familiar. It was the voice of Mr. Byron, one of the teachers at Carl Sandburg Elementary School.

"In the end, it turned out that Mr. Byron was pretending to be the ghost of Carl Sandburg.

"Carl Sandburg was a real-life writer who used to live in Chicago. Carl Sandburg Elementary School was named after him.

"The notes had stuff in them from Carl Sandburg's poems and short stories.

"Anyway, Mr. Byron used to be an

actor before he became a teacher. He sometimes liked to dress up in costumes and act stuff out to help the kids learn. He thought that pretending to be the ghost at Carl Sandburg and giving the kids a mystery to solve would help them learn about the person the school was named for.

"And Gerry and Tess solved the mystery!"

"The end," Nancy said. She glanced up from the purple notebook and took another deep breath.

The class burst into applause. Even Brenda was clapping a little. Mrs. Reynolds had a big smile on her face. So did Phoebe, Bess, and George.

"That was an excellent story," Mrs. Reynolds said. "Good work, girls." She added, "Let's see—the next team up will be Jason Hutchings's team. Jason?"

Jason rose from his desk and shuffled up to the front of the class. Nancy sat down at her desk and listened as Jason began reading a story about a mad science teacher at Carl Sandburg

Elementary School. The teacher, Mr. Bizzarobrain, was trying to make cats and rats morph into giant mutants that would take over the school.

Bess leaned across the aisle toward Nancy. "Cats and rats!" she whispered. "That's why George heard Jason and Mike talking about cats and rats."

"I guess so," Nancy replied, grinning.

Nancy settled back in her chair. As Mike read, her thoughts drifted to the mystery of the stolen purple notebook. All the loose ends were getting tied up.

She'd talked to Emily that morning about why she'd had two purple notebooks on Wednesday, and why she had acted so nervous about talking to Nancy. It turned out that not only had Emily had her team's purple notebook then, but one of her own that happened to look just like it.

Emily was nervous about talking to Nancy because Brenda had told her, Alison, and Jenny that Nancy's team would be trying to worm their story idea out of them. Brenda had said that they were not to talk to Nancy, Bess, George, or Phoebe about the short-story contest under any circumstances.

Nancy snapped to attention when Brenda got up to read *her* team's story. It was called "The Monster That Ate the State." It didn't have a whole lot to do with Carl Sandburg Elementary School except that the monster that ate the state they lived in happened to eat the school, too.

After Brenda, Andrew Leoni read a story about everyone's homework getting stolen. Then Julia Santos read a story about a bunch of art projects getting trashed. Then Mari Cheng read a story about someone's science experiment blowing up and turning all the kids and teachers purple. Finally, Katie Zaleski read a story about the principal getting kidnapped by aliens.

At the end of all the readings, everyone voted on the best story. After taking a tally of hands, Mrs. Reynolds announced: "And the winner is . . . Nancy Drew's team! Your story will be published in the next school newsletter."

"Yes!" Bess shouted. She and Nancy exchanged high fives. George and

Phoebe, across the room, were smiling happily.

Nancy turned to look at Brenda. She wasn't smiling at all.

Later at lunch, while Phoebe, Bess, and George were eating and talking about their big win, Nancy got out her blue detective notebook. She wrote:

I'm really glad we won first prize. Phoebe told Mrs. Reynolds about what she did, and she even told Brenda that she didn't have to sharpen pencils for her. So everything turned out okay.

Mrs. Reynolds said that writing stories is easier and more fun when you work as a team. It's really true.

Plus, it goes for solving mysteries, too!

Case closed.